Addicted To You

Melissa C

Published by Melissa Current, 2024.

ADDICTED TO YOU

First edition. February 2, 2024.

Copyright © 2024 Melissa C.

ISBN: 979-8224165353

Written by Melissa C.

Table of Contents

Chapter 1 Harper 1
Chapter 2 Harper 5
Chapter 3 Jax 9
Chapter 4 Harper 12
Chapter 5 Jax 15
Chapter 7 Harper 23
Chapter 8 Jax 28
Chapter 9 Harper 32
Chapter 10 Jax.. 36
Chapter 11 Harper... 39
Chapter 12 Harper... 44
Chapter 13 Jax.. 48
Chapter 14 Harper...52

I want to thank my family for always being there for me
and allowing me the freedom to write in my spare time.
I love you all. I hope I can continue to gain insperation
for more stories.

Chapter 1 Harper

S*mack*, his warm hand lands hard on my ass cheek and a wave of pleasure runs through my body. A loud moan escapes my lips followed by a breathy "Again". *Smack, smack,* His hand smacks down again and again, God it feels so fucking good. His hand rubs the heated skin on my ass then travels lower to settle between my legs on my bare cunt. I grasp the legs of the table I am bent over in anticipation of what's coming. Moans fall from my lips as his finger rubs on my aching clit. Cries of pleasure come as he slides his fingers into my hot folds and rubs my g spot. My wrists rub against the padded shackles while I struggle to hold still as pleasure races through my body.

A small whimper escapes my lips as his touch leaves me. He returns by taking a long slow lick and then sucking my clit into his mouth. He sucks vigorously, I feel myself close to release. *Smack,* His hand comes down again as his tongue attacks my clit, I scream out in pleasure as my orgasm rips through me and my body feels limp.

"I'm going to fuck you like the good little whore you are" he says, his husky voice full of lust and want.

"Please" I beg. I want him to fuck me; it has been far too long since I have had him.

I hear his belt and then his zipper, I groan with desire as I lay there shackled to the table waiting. I have waited for months to have this again, I am so tired of waiting, I am so desperate for another release. *Smack*, his hand lands hard down on my pussy, it makes me gasp but I follow it with a loud "more".

"Hold still for me baby cakes" he groans in my ear before thrusting his hard dick inside my pussy all the way to the hilt. He bucks his hips faster and harder as he wraps his hand in my long brunette hair and pulls my head back to give him better leverage.

"Yes. Fuck me" I moan "More" I cry out

"Be a good little whore for me" he says as he smacks my ass again

My pussy starts to spasm, I grasp the table legs, my arousal drips from me as my orgasm rocks through my body. He continues thrusting until he rides out his release and fills me, I lay there breathless.

"SO, ARE YOU STILL WITH him" Jax asks me with a raised brow and buttoning up his dark blue jeans.

"Yes" I tell him as I pull my navy-blue V-neck back on so I can fix my hair.

"Why do you stay with him Harper?" He asks trying to hide his annoyance.

"He's good to me Jax and he wants a relationship." I answer pulling out my curling iron to reset my long curls.

"Yet you call me when you want a good fuck" He whispers in my ear and gives my ass a squeeze as he walks by me on his way to my tiny kitchen to grab a beer.

His hot breath on my ear sends a spark of heat through my body and desire hits at my core again. I wouldn't have to seek him out for great sex if he wasn't so stubborn. I don't know why he has a hang up with relationships. Jax Adams had a stubborn streak a mile wide and the front of your typical bad boy. His tall and lean hard body connects to a set of broad shoulders and massive biceps. His hard frame is covered in tattoos adding to that sexy bad boy image complete with a bit of a rap sheet. His dark brown eyes turn almost black when they fill with desire. He drips with dominance and sex appeal making him just about the perfect specimen. I knew the real him though, he would dominate me in the bedroom, but he was gentle, and his heart was pure. Our sex was amazing, according to him he didn't want anyone else, he just refused to get any more serious than that and I wanted the title.

"That's because you satisfy me Jax, but Tony wants a girlfriend" I say matter of factly as if what I'm doing isn't fucked up in the least.

"Hey, I told you I didn't want to fuck anyone else but you baby cakes, but you got hung up on a stupid title." He says with his irritation front and center

"I want a boyfriend Jax, and I wanted you to spend more time not doing things that could get you thrown in jail. You know the deal." I confess, it wasn't all about the relationship, mostly though, but it was about him being reliable and stable, not in a jail cell. I know it was all petty crime stuff like paraphernalia and shoplifting, so when he did get busted, he never did much time, but the possibility of it all the time really sucked.

"Well, want in on hand baby cakes" he says as he walks over to me and places a firm hold on my throat. He leans in and takes my earlobe in between his teeth then gives it a soft suck before whispering, "Be a good whore and get on the bed," and I am all too eager to obey his command.

Chapter 2 Harper

I grab a lavender bath bomb from underneath my sink and toss it in the extra hot bath water I prepared. I am in desperate need of soothing my aching muscles, not to mention the tender skin on my ass. After the first round with Jax I was already sore, but the second one left me laying on the bed unable to move for an hour. I climb into the tub and sink down into the hot water; I let out a loud sigh as I feel the soothing water wrap around my skin. Holy fuck that was great, but I am going to feel it for a few days.

After taking my long soak in my tub, I pull on a black silk night dress, I can't handle anything to restrictive right now. I continue on with my Friday night routine which consists of popcorn, beer, and true crime documentaries. As I settle into my bed I smile and feel a hint of arousal start to creep in as I get a whiff of his musky smell that is lingering on my sheets. Fuck he always smells so damn good. I'm going to have to wash my sheets before Tony comes over again. I finally settle on a documentary and start shoving my face full of popcorn trying to fight of the desire to call Jax again. I know my poor body couldn't handle it, but arousal consumes me just the same.

"HARPER LYNN KENNEDY" I hear from the other end of the phone as soon as I answer it

"Hey Kellie" I say calmly. Fuck, the cats out of the bag now. I should have known that Jax wouldn't keep his mouth shut when it came to his sister. She wanted us to be together just as much as I did, sometimes more it seemed. Kellie was force of nature and always was a little outspoken. We've known each other since we were kids, and we were still close. I just still wanted to keep my cheating hook ups with her sexy ass brother a secret. Jax clearly didn't feel the same.

"Oh, don't you, hey Kellie me you sexy little slut. When the hell were you going to tell me, you were fucking my brother again?" she says playfully

"It's only every few months. Sometimes I just need him. It was staying a secret, but I guess he couldn't resist." I confess to her

"I still don't know why both of you can't get your heads out of your asses and figure out that you belong together." she says

"He just can't commit Kellie" I say trying not to sound too sad about it.

"Honey, only fucking you, and no one else is committed for an Adams man. That's like... a huge deal." Kellie reminds me. She has made that statement plenty of times and unfortunately it was true.

"You talk like it's a requirement for your family Kellie" I chuckle

"Well, what do you expect. They're like all criminals Harper not husbands, they run the risk of going to jail every day, they also love sex, it's just who they are." She says with her, it is what it is, attitude.

"You say that like you guys are a fucking no commitment, criminal sex club or some shit" I say with laughter.

"That's fucking hilarious, my dad would love that" she laughs "hey I'll come see you next weekend ok"

"k, bye" I say as I hang up. "Fucking Jax!" I say out loud as I rummage my medicine cabinet for some aspirin. Why the fuck did he blab to Kellie?

We have had this arrangement for a while now and I wanted it to stay a secret. The less people who know the better. A few years ago, when I gave up on the hope that Jax and I would be anything more two people who have fucking amazing sex together, I stopped going around. I kept in contact with Kellie, but I tried to keep some distance. That's when I met Tony. He was nice, clean cut, and I didn't have to worry about him ending up in jail. He wants a future with me, and he has the job to provide.

Jax always provided, I mean I never went without. I have my house because of him and my car. The house is small but it's mine, I own it. Until I met Jax I had never owned anything in my life. I guess everything I have is because of him in a way. He just never seemed to come by money in the legal way. With Tony everything is on the up and up. Well, everything except the sex.

Tony is stable, and predictable. He wants to be in a relationship with me, and it would be security if we were to ever have kids. I never had any of those things growing up. My family was fucked up. My dad was a junkie and absent most of the time and my mom wasn't much better. She drank all the time, had a new boyfriend every month or so, and we were always moving because she always ended up drinking away the rent. Jax and Kellie eventually convinced their family to take me in. They saved me, but that is still not the life I would want for any child.

I need the stability and less dysfunction, even if it comes with unfulfilling sex.

Chapter 3 Jax

"You fucking did what!" Kellie yells at me "I can't believe you Jax, What the fuck were you thinking"

"Don't be like that Kellie, you know I only want her" I say trying to justify my actions. I mean she calls me, but I always go running.

"Then all you had to do was be her boyfriend Jax." She snaps.

"Fuck Kellie, don't start with that! Why did we need a fucking label on it? Why do girls always have to fuck shit up with titles?" I say knowing that it really would have been that simple and I was diffidently way too stubborn, but so was Harper.

"Look, Jax, I understand in our family it's normal, I mean fuck, Mom and Dad still aren't married, but Harper has wanted "normal" since we were kids. So, she may be stubborn and ridiculous about it at times but that's her dream and she wanted that with you. She loves you, but she wanted commitment. She has that now." Kellie is stern in her words, but that shit eating grin she has on her face tells me she excited about it and no doubt heading outside to call Harper right now. I fucking hate it when she's right though, I probably should leave well enough alone but Harper's like a fucking addiction.

I probably shouldn't have told Kellie because I'm going to hear about it from Harper, but I had to tell somebody. Kellie and Harper were pretty close, so I was hoping to maybe see if there was any way to maybe win her back. I really can't resist her. She calls and I run to her, every time no matter what I'm doing. I know she's with Tony and he's safe and shit, but he can't satisfy her. My baby needs handled right, and I know how to do that, not fucking Tony. I don't know why she wastes her time with that guy anyway. That's a fucking lie, I know why, she's with him because I couldn't commit to anything more than fucking only her. I don't want to be with anyone else, and I haven't been. Not even in the in the first two years after Harper left. How's that for fucking commitment.

The first time she called my heart about beat right out of my chest. I was so nervous I almost stumbled over my words making an ass of myself. When she told me she needed to see me I was there, no questions asked. When I saw the tears in her eyes when she opened the door, I was ready for blood. I laughed out loud when she told me the tears were just form the lack of sexual pleasure for two years. When I gave her a hug for comfort and she leaned in and whispered "I'll be a good little whore for you" my dick got so hard I couldn't resist the urge to rip her skimpy, silk night gown right down the middle and hoist her up on my hips and suck her hardened nipple right into my mouth as I carried her to the bed.

It had been so long since I had her, I took my time. Kissing and biting every inch of her breasts, and then all the way down to her hot soaking wet pussy. I sucked her clit right into my mouth and I savored that shit. She wrapped her fingers up in my hair pulling me in closer to her sweet cunt. Uncontrollable moans fell from her lips as I traveled lower and licked around her ass, when I slid my fingers inside her dripping pussy I kept my thumb on her clit. Every bit of her was being ravished, I pumped my fingers vigorously as I sucked and licked her ass. Her pussy started to spasm around my fingers, and her release was soon dripping from her. I took my pants off as fast as I could, she was so ready for me to fuck her.

"Roll over" I commanded her, and my good girl obeyed.

I grabbed her hips and positioned her ass in the air. I lined my dick up in the center of her hot folds, I slid my finger up her pussy getting it wet, then I started rubbing soothing circles between her ass cheeks. With one hard thrust of my hips, I slammed my hard cock deep inside of her as I continue massaging her. I inched my finger inside and a pleasure filled "Yes" escaped her. I continued thrusting and fingering, her screams got louder and louder. I could feel my release coming soon.

"Harder, I'll be your good little whore" She moaned out and with her words I found my release. I rode out my orgasm and collapsed next to her on the bed. I pulled her in close to me and we drifted off to sleep.

It was from that point on we had an arraignment. When she really needed it and Tony was going to be away for a while Harper could call. I know it's wrong and fucked up, but I need her just as much as she needs me. I need to find a way to get her back, without a fucking title.

Chapter 4 Harper

I wake to the sound of my alarm ringing in my head. The bed groans as I sit up to find my slippers. I let out a yawn and I wince a little through it as the stretch that comes with it pulls my still incredibly sore muscles. I guess I'll be having aspirin with breakfast again. Today is welcomed, it's Monday so I can get back to work and have a good distraction from Jax. I have to get back to reality before Tony gets back to town. Today will be busy, it's the first day of October so that means we get to change everything over to our fall menu at the coffee shop I manage.

I love this time of year, the cool crisp air in the mornings, apple crisp and pumpkin spice everything, and the beautiful yellows and reds of the changing leaves. Everyone starts decorating with scarecrows, pumpkins and straw bales getting ready to kick off all the holiday craft fairs. My favorite part is the warm clothes. I get to get out all of my favorite hooded sweatshirts, flannels, cute hats and bear paw boots. Fall is probably my favorite season.

When I get to work, I am greeted with a smiling face and a hot pumpkin spice breve.

"Well, tell me what you think boss" Amy says cheerfully. I think she loves Fall just as much as I do

"Amy that's perfect, thank you so much!" I tell her after tasting her masterpiece.

"I couldn't wait! I just had to open the boxes and give the new stuff a try" She cheers "also, all the boxes are in the storeroom ready to be entered into the inventory and I pulled all the old menus. Oh, and I decorated the menu board for fall."

"Thank you. Let's get to work then" I cheer with excitement.

I HAD SPENT THE DAY decorating, changing over inventory, and deciding what the specials will be for the month I didn't even realize it was closing time. The shop looks pretty great, not to brag on myself or anything. It was such a welcomed distraction, but the Aspirin I took at lunch was starting to wear off and I could use a good hot bath. After a quick stop at the store for some necessities, also known as dinner from the deli, I make my way home.

After my not-so-great ready-made dinner I get my bath prepared. I go for a rose bubble bath paired with a glass of cheap wine and a movie on my phone. The warm water from the bath wraps around me, hugging every inch of my skin and a soothing sensation flows through my body. The rose bubbles offered up a relaxing aroma, breathing it in deep brought me peace. My little escape to paradise was soon interrupted by the sound of my text messages. I let out a groan of disappointment as I pick up my phone to see who it was. I want to ignore it, but I haven't heard from Tony his whole trip so far and I really don't want to miss his check in. My heart flutters in my chest a little when I see it's Jax.

Dammit he shouldn't get to me like that. My feelings betray me; there is no future with Jax. He doesn't want commitment. I want a husband and kids someday. Jax can't offer me that, especially not honestly. Jax and the other Adams men are known in the area for their shady lifestyle. Their shady pawn shops provide store fronts to sell all the merchandise they usually get by the "fell off the back of a truck" method. There are also their drug dealings, as if being thieves wasn't bad enough. I'm also pretty confident that the first car he got me was from his uncle's chop shop, maybe even the one I have now.

My shelter has been on behalf of his family in one way or another from the time I was 16. I had lousy parents and an unstable home life, I'm not even sure my mom ever noticed I was gone, I mean I don't recall her ever coming to look for me. They took me in, offered me a room and food, Kellie even stole me my clothes until I learned enough to do it myself. Jax's mom gave me my first cigarette, and his dad offered me my first beer. It was dysfunctional, but stable. There was love and kind words, it may have been praise for the good job you did stealing a TV or selling a bag of drugs, but it was kind just the same and made me feel wanted. I just can't understand why Jax could provide me with everything I wanted, a house, a car, furnishings, and even only having sex with me, but he couldn't commit to calling it a relationship.

Looking at the message he wrote sends my stomach into knots but a blush to my cheeks. I feel my body temperature rise enough that I am sure it could reheat my bath water. The message simply read:

Hey baby cakes. I have grown tired of our arrangement. I want you back and I will get what I want. I will get to shackle you to that table anytime I want.

I don't even know how to process that information.

Chapter 5 Jax

"Jax, did you and Hector get that car in last night?" Ricky asked as he opened the door, his voice echoed through the garage and pulled me from the tire I was changing.

"Ya, it's in the back" I yell back at him. My older brother Ricky helps my cousin Kenny run a tire shop, the heat was on my uncle Mick a few years back, so he had to shuffle things around. The tire shop runs a much more honest business. There is a warehouse out back where we keep the tire inventory, but it also serves as the intake for the other garages. I work here to part time so I can show an honest paycheck, and I run cars on the weekends for Kenny and Ricky. I started running cars after Harper left, I needed more of a thrill since I was majorly lacking sexual satisfaction. She poured her heart and soul into the coffee shop, became the manager and tried to convince herself that she didn't need me, while I took my crimes to the next level. My dad wants me to take over one of the pawn shops, but I don't know if I want that yet, or at all.

"Ok. Have it ready to move tonight!" He bellowed. If it wasn't for the fact that he's my brother and he has always come off as a loud fucking ass, I might have thought he was mad. He was 6' 3" and he was fucking built, that fucker lived at the gym. Those stupid muscle shirts he wore helped draw plenty of attention to him. The girls practically spread their legs on the spot for him, and he was always more than happy to accept the offers.

"Ya, ya, ya. I will." I mutter under my breath getting back to work.

"JAX, ARE YOU FUCKING sure about this?" Hector questions me as we start making preparations to move the car.

"Fuck ya!" I answer confidently

"Ok. It's just she's a good girl, she's not like us man. She's got a real job and everything" he says lightheartedly but there's an underlying seriousness in his voice.

"I've got to get her back Hector. She's all I want." I say knowing that he's going to give me his honest opinion and I may not like it. That is why I talk to him though. Hector and I go way back to grade school, we grew up together, hell we even went to jail together. He's honest and lets me know what's up. He was there for me when Harper left, let me sleep on his couch for a while even.

"I'm just saying she deserves to be happy and have a good life is all" he says, and I know his concern for her Is genuine.

"She also deserves to be pleasured the way she wants; she shouldn't have to hide that side of her!" I say and the words come out a little more frustrated than I would like.

"How the fuck do you know she's not?" he questions with a sharp tone and his brows furrowed

"Because I'm the one who's been doing it." I confess bracing for the earful I am about to get.

"You're Fucking sleeping with her again! What the fuck are you thinking Jax?" He starts scolding me and it makes me feel like a child. "Why the fuck would you do that. She has a boyfriend who wants a future with her. That's all Harper has ever wanted Jax it can't just be about sex." He continues, his tone is firm, and his face is scowled in disappointment. It makes me angry, but I listen.

"She fucking called me, first off, and I do want a future with her dammit!" I yell, emotions flaring "I bought her a fucking house, I lived with her, I got her a reliable car so she could get downtown because she wanted a real job. I wanted her and only her, I just didn't want to put a fucking label on it. Why the fuck is that so wrong?" I say unloading on Hector as if he's the reason for losing Harper. It's my fault, I know it is, but I don't like it when it gets pointed out she moved on to Tony, if that's even what you want to call it.

"The label means the world to her Jax. To her that means commitment and stability. I told you she's not like us. She had a shit life, and we got her into some shit situations, but she is good and wants a good life." He pauses for a moment before continuing on with probably the most valid question of the night.

"What the fuck can you really offer if you don't want to call it what it is and clean up your life a little. Does she even know you're here, helping the chop shop? Honest answer Jax." He asks, his tone softer but his expression lets me know he can see through any bullshit I try to feed him right now. I know he's right but that doesn't make it hurt less.

I offer him a simple "no" because it's the truth. Harper doesn't know I'm here; she would fucking kill me. She wanted me to stay out of jail and this, this is actual time in prison, not a few weeks here or there in county. I know I should listen to him, he's right. I don't bring much stability to the table and asking her to consider raising kids while I'm in and out of jail isn't fucking very fair, but I fucking love her, I have since we were young. I have to let her know that that's better than any fucking label, that's fucking real shit.

"We better get back to work" Hector says offering me a smile and handing me the tool bag.

Chapter6 Harper

"Who the fuck does he think he is" I say to myself as I shuffle through the end of the night receipts and paperwork that cover my desk. What the fuck is Jax thinking. He interrupted my bath, and then my sleep two nights in a row, now I can't even concentrate on my work. I don't even know what to think about it all, he can't commit so why would he want me back. Tony is due to be home tonight and Jax is supposed to leave me alone after a good fuck. He is supposed to stay out of sight until I get a wild horny hair and call him again, not tell his fucking sister about it and make it public knowledge. He was sure as hell not supposed to decide to change our agreement. My stomach stirs and the knots grow stronger, there was so much unpredictability now, what if he shows up, what if he tells Tony? I grab some club soda and some flavoring in hopes that an Italian soda will help calm my stomach. I grab my jacket and lock up for the night deciding that the paperwork can wait until morning.

The soda and the drive home seem to help calm my nerves, but I am still upset. Why does he think he can just decide now to fuck up a good thing? It's not the right thing to be doing but it's an arrangement that I can live with. I get to have a future with commitment and stability without criminal charges lingering, as well as a much-needed hard kinky fuck. Neither man can seem to offer me both, otherwise I wouldn't be in this position.

When I pull into my driveway I am surprised when I see Tony's car on the street. I didn't think he would be back in town until later tonight and he usually spends his first night home at his apartment in the city. I am greeted at the door with flowers, Roses to be exact and a bottle of expensive wine.

"Hey Hun, how was your week?" Tony asks with his award winning bright white smile, we had been together for a while before I learned he had spent the money to get veneers, he said he wanted to look his best in his photo for his business card. I guess when you sell luxury apartments in the cities you want to look your best. I admit he is a handsome man; he is clean cut with piercing blue eyes and a sharp Jaw. His blond hair was kept short, and he kept his small frame covered in suits and preppy sweaters. Handsome, yes, Jax Adams sexy, no.

"It was good, I did a lot of decorating at the shop and got everything switched over for fall, so it was productive. Thank you for the flowers." I say with a warm smile. I do love the flowers, Lilies are my favorite, but Tony thinks they aren't as romantic as roses. I have never been big on fancy expensive wine, but the gesture is sweet. He tries, and I appreciate it.

I start nervously rummaging through my kitchen to find a vase to put the roses in. Tony is here with both roses and wine; he is also still in his suit. Something is up I just know it. He never wears his Ralph Lauren, or Armani, or whichever fucking stupid designer he's wearing, I never gave a fuck about any of that shit. He won't even wear them of dates, he always tells me it's because I don't have anything to wear that would come close to matching it, at the same time reminding me he could buy something for me if I was worried about the price. I usually just try to play it off as I'm too proud to accept it instead of telling him that I am just not into that fucking shit, and the fact he thinks it's about money is slightly insulting. I want stability, I don't want to look stuck up and superficial, I am a jeans and leggings type of girl. I finally find where I stashed my vase and prepare the water for the roses when Tony places a piece of paper on the counter and tells me to look at it.

"What's this?" I ask looking at a paper with a beautiful luxury apartment listing on it. It had a huge open floor plan that was naturally lit by huge windows that showcased the stunning view of the city. The kitchen was huge and full of stainless-steel appliances to match the gray tones of the paint and the floors. The master bathroom had a gorgeous walk-in shower with a waterfall shower head, in the corner was a beautiful sunken jacuzzi tub that I could almost envision myself soaking in right now. The walk-in closet looked like it was the size of a whole bedroom, I could never fill that thing. It was a beautiful place, but didn't give a very homey feel.

"Do you like it?" Tony asks almost giddy

"Well, it's beautiful and huge" I start to explain and am quickly cut off by Tony before I can even finish my thought

"Good, because I just bought it for us!" He exclaims

"You what?" I question him almost chocking on the words

"I looked at it this week while I was in Seattle" he says so proudly

"I-I-It's in Seattle" I stumble over the words trying to process what the fuck he is saying. I don't understand, why would he buy an apartment in Seattle for us, especially without talking to me first. I have told him I love it here, I love my job, and I love living outside of the city.

"Yes, Isn't it great!" He says as he pours us each a glass of the expensive wine he brought. He hands me one and extends his up in an attempt to toast.

"Oh, ya great." I say flatly "So you are moving?" I question looking for more answers and explanation

"No silly, we are moving. I transferred so I don't have to travel so much." he says gulping down the whole glass of wine he poured seemingly in one swallow. "Isn't that awesome!" He cheers

"Uh...Ya sure...Uh, can I take some time to process this all please. I mean that's a lot, I have a job and a house, and my friends." I say starting to feel panic rise and my stomach fall and knot up again. I don't really want to fight right now though so I throw in "It is just such a big surprise honey" and give him a hug and a kiss on the cheek.

"Alright, sweetie." He says giving me a small kiss "It's going to be great. We can start fresh, hardly any packing required. I'll see you tomorrow ok." He says as he heads to the door.

"Right. Tomorrow." I say as I close the door. What the actual fuck, I feel slightly betrayed, was he even thinking of me at all. I don't want to move, I don't want to live in a fancy apartment in the city, he really should know that I've mentioned that before, we stay at my place most of the time because of it. Fuck, this day just needs to be over.

Chapter 7 Harper

"Any plans after work tonight?" Amy cheerfully asks as she pulls her pink zip up jacket on preparing to leave for the night. She was always so cheery and bright, like nothing could ever drag her down. She was about the best barista I had. I was drawn to her bubbly, easygoing personality from the second she stepped in here for the interview and I am so grateful I hired her. She lives in pink; she also makes it her mission to put a smile on everyone's face. She always gets amazing reviews from the customers and keeps staff entertained and motivated. I was so excited when the owner and I came up with new designs for out uniform tee shirts. I got to order them in more colors than just black and gray, so I made sure to add pink as well as navy blue. The look on her face was priceless when she opened up the box and realized she could choose pink. She will make an amazing manager someday, I guess maybe sooner than I was thinking.

"Not really, just my usual Friday night, bubble bath, popcorn and true crime" I chuckle. When really, I know it will be another sleepless night and avoiding an important talk with Tony. He is still waiting for me to answer him, and I really don't want to.

"You and your true crime addiction" she laughs as she heads out of the shop.

I finish getting everything ready for the crew that will be in tomorrow morning and gather my things. As I walked outside the autumn breeze brought a pink color to my cheeks, it moved through my hair as it danced through the trees, I paused for a moment to enjoy the feeling. It was so beautiful this time of year with the leaves changing colors and falling as the trees prepare to sleep. As I make my way to my car I pull out my phone, just out of curiosity, to check the weather for Seattle...fucking rain, who would have fucking guessed.

AS I SOAK IN THE HOT water letting the bubbles tickle my skin and breathing in their warm fragrance of lilacs it takes me back to the early summer when I was 18. It was warm that night, the sky was filled with gorgeous hints of pink and orange as the sun started to set. Jax's dad had sent the boys on an errand for the pawn shop, Kellie and I tagged along to provide a distraction while Jax and Hector got out with some electronics. Things went smooth at the first store, and we made a successful drop at the shop. The next store didn't go as smooth; we ended up being chased by the cops. Jax grabbed me by the arm pulling me to the car. We lost the cops, but we also lost Hector and Kellie as well. We ended up out in the middle of nowhere alone.

We needed to lay low for a while, so we had plenty of time to talk. Jax shared some stories of when him and hector were in grade school and they had me laughing so hard. It seemed the Adams boys were just born to be a bit rough and rowdy. They had the wrong side of the track's reputation, but nobody ever really fucked with them. They were never afraid to fight and usually came out on the winning side. But if they were close to you and accepted you, you got to know a whole different side of them, the softer side.

After talking and smoking some weed on the hood of the car for what seemed like hours, admiring the way the stars looked in the summer sky, Jax confessed to something that took me by surprise but set my heart and body on fire. He told me that he had been crushing on me for a while now and wanted to kiss me. I was so nervous, he was so sexy, I was so afraid that I would mess it up. That first kiss was fire; it sent an aching sensation straight to my center. It was like instant chemistry. His rough hands explored my body, but they felt soft and gentle, his touch was magic and sent sparks through me.

His kisses started to travel lower, eventually landing on my neck, it ignited my belly with a desire I had never felt before. I wanted him, I needed him, in that moment I had to have him, all of him. With his hand caressing my breast, and open mouth kisses on my neck soft moans fell from my lips that I couldn't control. My core felt hot and wet, lust filled my eyes, I locked my gaze on his dark brown eyes and all I could breathe out was "Please". A lust filled groan is all he replied with to the permission I had just granted him.

His hands moved lower and grabbed the button on my jeans, once my zipper was opened his hand slid down into my black lace panties. My breath hitched in my throat as his finger found my clit.

"More" I begged, and he was more than happy to give it.

He slid my pants down and pulled me closer to the edge of the hood. He started planting soft kisses up my legs. I was so ready for him to ravage me. He took a long slow lick, I couldn't hold in my pleasure, I had never felt this before, loud pleasure filled moans escaped me as he sucked my clit into his mouth. I didn't want it to end but when he slid his two fingers into my warm folds and pumped them while his tongue worked my clit I couldn't help but find my release.

He laid beside me and crashed his lips against mine, and I parted my lips to allow his amazing tongue to slip in. His kiss was so full of passion it made me ache for more. I ran my fingers down his chest to his belt. I undid his buckle, then the button on his jeans, I gasped a little when I felt his hardened cock for the first time. Soft moans escape him as my hand pumped up and down. I felt his hot breath at my ear, and it was electrifying, he simply whispered "can I fuck you baby cakes?"

Through heavy panting a simple "ya" is all I could whimper. I was so overtaken by lust in that moment I felt tipsy and unable to think straight I just knew I need to feel more of him. He dropped his pants and lined his hard dick up at my center, he inched in slowly, I winced in pain, but it felt so fucking good.

"You ok baby" He asked with genuine concern in his voice

"Yes, please don't stop" I said reassuring him.

He kept his movements slow and steady at first and I moaned out with pleasure. He leaned in and sucked my nipple into his mouth and a whimper fell from my lips. His pace quickened and every kiss was filled with intensity, it was raw, and it was magic. My moans were timed to his thrusts, and my breathing grew faster, I felt like I was going to explode.

"More Jax" I scream out feeling myself right on the edge of release. He placed the pad of his thumb on my hardened nub and my release came uncontrollably. My toes curled, my head fell back, and my body went numb, I held him close to me as he rode out his release.

My thighs clench tightly and the bath water almost spills over the side of my tub as I find my release to the memory of our first time, my first time. Every sexual awakening I have ever had was at the hands of Jax Adams. The first time he smacked my ass I was so embarrassed that I liked it so much.

My phone pings and pulls me from my thoughts. I stand up to pull my soft black robe over my wet shoulders and step out onto my bathmat. Sliding my feet into my matching slippers, my chest rises and falls as I take a deep breath, not sure if I am prepared to see who it was that messaged me. My heart flutters a little bit, and a blush rises to my cheeks as I read his message:

Hey Baby Cakes! I can't wait to Fuck You again. I'm thinking a surprise visit may be in order. My dick is getting hard just thinking of your naked body bound and spread for me.

Chapter 8 Jax

I send the message knowing that it would get to her. We excite each other and neither one of us can deny that. I grab a towel so I can shave and take a shower. I'm getting a little scruffy and I want to look good for my girl. She likes it when I keep my goatee trimmed up, and she gets wet for my cologne. I know what turns her on and I am going to use that to my advantage right now. I can't risk that fuck face Tony winning. Harper is mine, she has always been mine, from that very moment I took her on the hood of my old car that night. She was amazing, she tasted amazing, she was pure. I was her first and I felt fucking honored, Harper Kennedy was fucking gorgeous, she had long brown hair, and her hazel eyes would intoxicate you when you looked into them. She only stood about 5'4" but she had a slender waist and a luscious ass. She could have had so many guys, but she wasn't like that.

I wasn't even sure she was going to let me kiss her that night, but I desperately wanted to try. I thought I was a lucky guy when I got to taste her sweet lips. She kissed me with such passion and desire, I had never been kissed like that before, it was like electricity sparking through my body. The way she looked into my eyes that night and asked "please" filled my body with lust and desire, it made my dick instantly hard, and I craved her. I was addicted to her, to the chemistry we had, to the lust I saw in her eyes at that moment. I have to get her back, I must!

I SNEAK IN QUIETLY since I don't see that assholes car out front. She looks so fucking sexy sleeping in that short red silk night gown, it doesn't cover her ass all the way, so I have a perfect view of her red lace panties. Her ass looks so inviting, I pull my pants off to free my hard cock. The bed groans as I climb in next to her, I run my hands up her legs and stop at her ass. I lean in slowly and take her earlobe in my mouth to take a hard suck. I whispered in her ear "I'm going to fuck you baby cakes!"

"I was expecting you" was her only reply as she rolled to gain access to my lips. I climb on top of her and pin her arms above her head as I slowly nibble at her neck and her collar bone. I let my mouth slowly travel down to her breasts and soft moans fall from her lips as I suck on her pebbled nipple. I release her hands so I can travel lower, I need a taste of that sweet pussy of hers. Her fingers tangle in my hair and a breathless "yes" escapes her as I move her panties to the side and take a long languid lick. Fuck she tastes so good. I take her clit between my tongue and my teeth; she pulls on my hair but holds me closer wanting more.

I lick and suck at her clit as I slide my fingers inside her hot folds thrusting them hard and fast like she likes. I listen with pride as her uncontrollable moans keep coming. I want to send her over the edge so I do something I know will get to her. I move my mouth to her ass attacking it with my tongue and place my thumb on her clit, she screams out in pleasure as all of her is being ravaged. Her release comes in waves, her hands pull my hair, her toes cure and her thighs try to clench, "OH FUCK" she screams as she drips with the pleasure, I just gave her. I chuckle with delight knowing that I am the only one that can give her this.

As she catches her breath I go to the closet to get some rope, I haven't tied her hands to the bed in a while, and I know she likes it. I toss the red velvet rope on the bed next to her and command her to roll over. Her eyes fill with lust and her lips curl up into her perfect smile.

"I promise I'll be a good little whore" she says rolling over and extending her hands to the headboard. Fuck, I love it when she talks like that.

With her hands tied to the bed and her lush ass propped up for me, I am ready to tease her. *Smack*, my hand comes down on her ass cheek.

"More" she groans softly as my hand connects with her ass again.

I take a long hard lick of her sweet pussy, and it clenches a little as she braces for what she knows is coming.

"Yes" she screams as my hand smacks against her soaking center "Again" she screams "please", and I refuse to disappoint her.

It makes me so hard, and I want nothing more than to slam my dick into her right fucking now, but I fight that urge. My baby likes to beg, and this night is about her. I have to do anything I can to get Harper back, so I will be patient and wait for her. She may be bound but she is the one in control. *Smack*, my hand makes contact again and again, finally the words fall from her lips "Please Jax, fuck me."

At her request I ready my dick at her dripping folds and dig my fingers into her hips.

"How baby cakes" I ask hoping she will give the answer I am longing for.

"Hard! Please, I fucking need you" she pants. My lips curl into a smile, that was exactly the answer I wanted.

With one hard thrust I fill her walls all the way and hard moans escape us both. She feels so fucking good. My nails dig into her skin as my grip gets tighter and tighter. My pace quickens as I slam into her over and over, faster and faster. She screams out my name as her pussy spasms, I feel her release dripping all over. I fucking love it when I do that to her. I keep my pace quick and my breathing changes as I feel myself about to let go. My head falls, and my toes start to tingle as I fell myself filling her fully. We collapse on the bed, out of breath and fulfilled. I untie the rope and pull Harper's naked body against mine and without even thinking about it I whisper "I love you" before drifting off to sleep.

Chapter 9 Harper

I can't even open my mouth to respond, did he really just say that, better yet did he really mean it. Jax has never said "I love you" to me before, ever. It always comes in the form of "you are mine" or "I only want you." It makes me want him; it makes me miss what I had with him and makes me feel very conflicted. I know I have to answer Tony, and a part of me thinks I should move with him. It is safe, reliable, and the apartment really is beautiful. There is another part of me that thinks I love it here, maybe Jax really will commit to me, maybe it just took him a while to grow up, and also maybe I was too hard on him. He said he loves me, maybe the stupid title really doesn't matter, he loves me, that's probably enough, no that is enough. I sink down into his arms and join him in sleep.

I AM AWAKENED BY THE sound of Jax's phone, I am sleepy, but I overhear part of the conversation.

"Hey Jax, I know its late, but Kenny may have a run for you tomorrow, can you give Hector a heads up?" I recognize the voice on the other end of the line. It's Ricky, but what does he mean by run?

"Ya, no problem, man. I'll catch up with you tomorrow" Jax says hanging up the phone.

"What was that about?" I ask Jax with furrowed brows

"Well, I may need to fill in and help Ricky" Jax says nervously like he wants to hide something

"Fill in how Jax" I push

"Baby, um" Jax starts to explain, and I already know where this is heading. What the hell is he thinking? That's fucking prison time!

"Are you fucking kidding me Jax!" I yell. I could fucking kill him right now. He tells me he loves me just for me to find out he wants to go run cars what the fuck!

"Baby, please don't be like that. I don't have to do it anymore; Hector can handle it" he says trying reach for me.

"Anymore, what the fuck does that mean?" I scowl. How fucking long has he kept this from me? Why did he keep this from me? A feeling of betrayal washes over me.

"Hector and I help on the weekends some. It gave me a rush. I primarily work honestly now though I swear." he says trying to smooth things over

"A rush! What kind of fucking rush are you going to get in fucking prison Jax! You could get years for that!" I say with a belly full of anger and a chest full of hurt. I can't believe he is risking being apart for that long. My heart breaks at the thought of losing him like that and I am so angry that he would play such a risky game.

"I'm always careful baby cakes. I don't have to do it anymore. Kenny said they have a full-time position at the tire shop and its mine if I want it, it would be all honest work for us." He says and I know he Is just trying to reassure me, but I am so overwhelmed with emotion it's like I can't control it.

"How could you fucking do this to me Jax? You told me you loved me for the first time ever, you insist that you want to win me back, but you are fucking do this. You are playing with my emotions right now! You are a fucking ass hole!" I scream at him unable to stop any word vomit that might decide to escape my lips.

"I'm sorry, do fucking what to you exactly Harper? I fucking love you! You fucking left me! You moved someone else right on into your bed! I didn't do that shit. I haven't fucked anyone else since that fucking night with you on the hood of my car! You chose to not have a fucking say so in my fucking life anymore! If anyone is playing with anyone's emotions Harper Kennedy its fucking, you!" He says harshly and it fucking hurt. Deep down I knew it was true, but I am too stubborn to admit any wrongdoing right now.

"You have to have emotions to play with in the first fucking place Jax! If you really loved me, you would have committed to me, you would have called it what it was! The only person you care about is yourself!" I say harshly, I see his face fall like I crushed him, and I instantly regret it. That was fucked up and I know it.

"Fuck you Harper! I have always loved you, I didn't want a label, but you did, fine I get it, but I never meant that I didn't want to spend every day of my life with you. I'm done running to you at your whim and not getting to have you, it hurts to fucking bad." He says as his voice breaks and with one swift slam of my door he was gone.

My tears are relentless, falling with the intensity of a summer rainstorm. What the fuck did I just do. I think I just lost Jax for good and I have nobody to blame but myself. I never should have said those things to him. It doesn't change the fact that he should have told me, or that he never should have been helping the stupid shop. What the fuck was he thinking. Anger rises again and I can't take this anymore.

I pull my red silk robe on over my shoulders and tie it; I grab my phone and head to my kitchen. After pouring myself a glass of the expensive wine Tony left the other day, I take a look around my tiny house, I love it so much, but everything is Jax here. Maybe a fresh start wouldn't be bad. Maybe I need to move on fully. If I have lost him for good, then maybe I just need to let go of all the reminders I have of him. Like Tony said a fresh start, I assume his no packing required comment was a nice way of saying my stuff was shit, but it would be a smooth transition that way. Polishing off a second glass of wine and fulled by pain and anger I pick up my phone and open my messages. I scroll to Tony and decide to give him and answer

Hi Hun, Sorry it's so late. It was just such a shock I needed time to process it. I think Seattle will be nice. We can talk about it over lunch on Monday. You can come by the shop if you would like.

Chapter 10 Jax

I am fucking crushed. How the fuck could she say that I don't have feelings. I fucking live for her. She calls and I fucking run every fucking time. She wanted a house I fucking bought her one. I saved for a long time for that shit. Ever since I met Harper I was drawn to her. She was beautiful and she was kind. She worked hard in school; I think it brought a welcomed distraction from her fucked up home life. She never let her struggles show to most. Kellie and I knew what was going on though. Finally, when she was 16 we had the opportunity to help her. Her fucking mom never even came to look for her, never reported her missing, I don't even know if she even cared enough to notice Harper wasn't there anymore.

I wanted the best for her always. She was able to get out of the life. She told me she wanted a normal job so I made sure she could do that. I made sure Uncle Mick knew what I needed, and he came through. Harper was so happy the day she came home and told me she got the job at the coffee shop; it made me so proud. I was fucking hurt when she left, we were both so stubborn. She never could get over the fact I wouldn't call her my girlfriend, and I wasn't willing to cave. I fucked it up then and I fucked it up again.

"I'LL TAKE CARE OF THE car tonight man, don't worry about it" Hector reassures me with a little too much sympathy wearing on his face

"Thanks" I say a little more flatly than I wanted to

"You going to take that full time job Kenny has open?" he asks softly almost as if he's hoping I will.

"I don't know man, if I don't have Harper to think about, I might just take over a store for my dad. I don't know" I confess. I really don't know what I want to do. I had a plan to go on the up and up for her now, I don't know.

"I think you should, it's a good job." he states his opinion but with concern

"I don't know I'll think on it for a while now. Thanks for taking care of the car." I tell him as I head to the door to leave

"Hey Jax," He stops me before I can head out

"Ya" I say turning to face him

"Are you really done running to her?" he asks with his brow cocked

"Ya. It just hurts too fucking bad to keep doing it" I say and my heart clenches in my chest at the thought of never seeing her again

"Are you in love with her?" he asks

"Yes, I am." I tell him turning back to the door

"Then fight for her, go clean and prove to her you want to be there for her. Don't Just fucking give up like that man" he says, I nod my head to him as I close the door behind me.

Maybe Hector is right, maybe I should clean up my life a little. The money from the cars was crazy good though. Maybe I could take over the pawn shop my dad wants me to but run it straight. I don't know how much it really matters at this point. I pissed Harper off, and I don't think she will ever take me back. I told her she had no say so in my life anymore and made it sound like I thought she was a slut or something. She got with Tony, but it wasn't right away, and she hasn't been with anyone else other than me. She wasn't the kind of girl to sleep around, she formed very specific kinky likes, but she wasn't a slut, I never should have made it sound that way. She has every right to be pissed at me.

On the other hand, she was the one that left though, and then when she wasn't satisfied, she called me but only for the sex. I am so fucking hurt, but I let her do it. I knew what she needed so I let her use me for it. It was great for a while, but jealousy is a fickle mistress. I needed her more and more. I guess I used her in ways too, maybe things would have played out differently if I had turned her down. If I would have offered only comfort that night instead of letting us give into our sexual desires maybe I wouldn't be in this mess, but I am so fucking addicted.

I am addicted to her passion, not just in the bedroom, but the passion she puts into everything she does. I am addicted to her big gorgeous hazel eyes and the way they darken and fill with lust when she wants me to fuck her, but also the way they sparkle and light up her whole face when she is happy. I can't get enough of those beautiful sexy lips that curl into a perfect smile, and the way they look wrapped around my dick when she sucks me dry. Harper Kennedy is my drug, my addiction, her beauty and innocence pulls me in and the pleasureful high keeps me hungry for more. I don't think I will ever be able to walk away, no matter how much it fucking hurts to stay.

Chapter 11 Harper

I woke up Monday morning feeling a little apprehensive about the decision I had made over the weekend. I know it's not the right one especially because it was made in anger and hurt. I am still so mad at Jax for his actions, but his words, they fucking crushed me. I pull my fuzzy black robe over my shoulders and tie it; I slip on the matching slippers and head to the kitchen. I need coffee now instead of waiting until I get to work. I prepare my French press and start the kettle, my eyes drift to the view from my kitchen window. The apple tree that Jax planted for me my first year here has grown a lot, it even has put on apples a few years now. My lilly garden is slightly overgrown and neglected. I have been so busy it's been hard to keep up, but it is beautiful in the summertime.

The whistle of the kettle pulled me back to the task at hand, my coffee. I pour the boiling water into the French press and let it steep while I take care of the hot mess of a head I have going on right now. I decide I'm not feeling like putting in much effort today, so I keep things to a minimum. I run a brush through my long brown hair, pull it into a messy bun and wash my face. I throw on a little mascara and some clear lip gloss. I rummage through my closet to find something warm and cozy. I settle on a dark gray hoodie with the company logo on the back and a pair of dark blue jeans, I toss them on the bed for later.

I grab a coffee cup out of the cupboard and press down the lid to the French press. A little pumpkin cheesecake syrup mixed with some half and half; it was heaven in a cup. The steam warmed my cheeks as I took my first sip, the aroma woke my senses and as I drank it, it warmed my soul. Coffee really is my favorite part of the morning, and for the last several years this tiny kitchen is where I have enjoyed it. The thought of leaving it makes me feel empty.

I TURN THE MUSIC UP loud on my morning commute trying to avoid the voice in my head that is screaming at me. The screaming realization that I just made what is probably the worst decision of my life, and I have made some really bad decisions in the past. I have chosen to try to erase an entire chapter from my life for a man I care about but truly do not love. I don't want to think about it right now so avoidance will be my tactic today, until Tony shows up for lunch anyway.

As I struggle to find a parking spot at the coffee shop, I get a little excited, I guess my half price muffin Monday idea worked. I greet Amy as I walk in and visit with a few of the regulars before I head to the office to put my things down.

"Need any help Amy" I ask as I set my things in the office

"Ya actually, Crystal just threw in another batch of Pumpkin muffins, but I think we will need some apple and blueberry too. I needed Greg to help with drinks." She cheers, completely unaffected by the rush

"No problem, consider me on muffin duty." I say with a smile

I was so busy with the muffins I didn't have any time to think or pay attention to the time so I was surprised when Greg came to tell me I had a visitor. Knots turned in my stomach as I walked to the lobby, I felt a hint of relief when I saw that it was just Kellie.

"Hey Kellie, you want a coffee?" I ask seizing the opportunity for a coffee break

"Sure, you know I'll never turn that down" she laughs

"Ok, grab that corner booth and I'll meet you there" I say pointing to one of few tables left available. I get Amy started on making us one of her signature creations and hang up my apron. After grabbing two muffins and our coffee I head to the table to sit with Kellie.

"Sorry I didn't make it over this weekend; I had a date." she says boastfully

"It's ok...wait, what...with who?" I ask with excitement and curiosity

"Hector" she whispers with glee.

"Are you fucking serious" I was so excited for her, I always thought they would be good together but neither of them ever went for it. "How did that happen?" I ask

"Well, my dad has been looking for other business ventures and Hector mentioned that there was a bar for sale downtown. My dad thought that Hector and I could run it if it pans out. We ended up going to look at it together, before I knew it, he was telling me how beautiful he thought I was and asking me on a date." she tells me

"That's fucking crazy! To you and Hector." I say raising my coffee

"It was just one date so far, but he did kiss me at the end, and he's been texting me...a lot" she says with a smile that lights her eyes and makes her face glow.

"I'm happy for you. The two of you make sense, at least I think so." I say offering her a warm smile. "Is he a good kisser?" I ask with a laugh

"So fucking good!" She giggles as a blush shows in her cheeks. We share a moment of laughter together, but I knew a different topic would be brought up. It was only a matter of time.

"What's up with you and Jax?" she finally asks

"We had a fight. He doesn't want to see me anymore." I say as tears threaten to prick my eyes.

"What about?" she asks, blatantly prying

"I found out he was running cars for Kenny and Ricky" I say with annoyance creeping back in.

"Oh ya, that. Harper you do realize that when it comes to you, he's like a junkie right? He's fucking addicted, when you left, he didn't jump into bed with someone else he found a different drug all together, he needed another rush." She says as if it made him justified in his actions. The statement also seemed to come as a bit of a passive aggressive jab towards me.

"It still makes me mad Kellie. He could go to prison for that. It's not just small-time stuff. I just can't believe he would risk that; we would be apart for so long." I say unable to hide my frustration

"You have to actually be together to be apart Harper. His risk was his own." she says directly and it fucking stings to hear. "Look, you are my best friend and always will be, but I've just got to say it. You and Jax both need to stop being so fucking stubborn. You love each other you need to fucking figure it out." The words hurt and I hate that she said them.

"Look, he said he's done with me. So, I have decided to move to Seattle with Tony. It will probably be better this way." I tell her trying to act confident in my decision.

"Are you fucking serious Harper. Seattle? What the fuck are you going to do in Seattle?" She asks obviously annoyed and shocked by the news, she also had a point, I had no fucking clue what I was going to do there.

"It's just the best option. It will be stable and predictable. I need that." I tell her sounding more like I am trying to convince myself instead of her

"So, you're just going to give up, leave just like that. Give up on love all because why... your parents fucking sucked. What fucking good is stability if there isn't love with it?" she says with disappointment

"I have to go Kellie, you just don't understand. Jax and I are done." I say desperately trying to fight back tears.

"He's fucking in love with you Harper, he will never be done with you! You fucking know it too but choose to ignore it, as if the title is what makes it real." she says bluntly as she gathers her things to leave "Thanks for the coffee" she adds as she leaves.

I was hoping the conversation would have gone better but it went about like I expected. Kellie pointed out my flaws and stubbornness, but she was right, my parents were fucked up and I created a fantasy of what I wanted in life, but it looks like I may have left out a key element in that. How good was my life really going to be if I didn't love who I was with?

Chapter 12 Harper

A relaxing sigh leaves me as I sink down into the hot bath water. It has been an emotional week full of tension, and I am feeling it. I haven't heard form Jax at all, not that I really expected to, but I guess I was hoping. I feel empty without him around, I miss his touch, his smell, he wasn't the only one who was addicted. He was every bit my drug as I was his and I have no clue how I will go on without him. I get more and more sick to my stomach every day that goes by. I know I have made the wrong choice and now I don't know how to fix it. The two people I care about the most aren't speaking to me, and Tony is so wrapped up in moving that he hasn't even noticed that I have hardly spoken to him, or that he's stood me up for 3 lunch dates now.

My phone pings interrupting my attempt at some relaxation, I debate not even looking at it, but curiosity gets the better of me. I feel a little disappointed when I see its just Tony.

Is the door open?

yes

I hear Tony walk in and start making himself at home, I'm not sure what he's doing out there exactly but it is not helping me relax. I get out of the bath and wrap my body up in a towel. I dry off and throw on some comfy pj's so I can see what he is up to.

"What are you doing?" I ask trying to hide my annoyance at the intrusion

"I'm taking pictures and measurements; you should probably clean up your dinner dishes." Tony says as he tries to rearrange things

"Why are you doing that?" I ask as my annoyance starts to turn to complete irritation.

"Well, I'm listing the house, and the movers will be here in a week to move my furniture." He says like I should already know, but he hasn't fucking been including me in any of the planning

"A fucking week...Tony, I thought we were going to talk about this, and why are you listing my house?" I blurt out not even trying to hide emotion

"We did talk. I told you I bought an apartment in Seattle, you messaged and said Seattle sounds nice. I told you we are starting over, so we will take my furniture, and you can pack a suitcase. Oh, and I found a buyer for your car." He said it like it was no big deal

"I assumed I had more time. I haven't even talked to the coffee shop yet; I was also never told I couldn't take my car. I wasn't planning on selling my house either. Dammit Tony did you even think of me at all in any of this?" I say as I feel myself starting to spiral.

"Let's be real Harper, your car is crap and most likely came from that shady ass garage anyway, I'll get you a better one." His statement angers me, shady garage or not it was mine, who the fuck does he think he is.

"It's still mine Tony. I own it, why wouldn't you ask me, and why are you trying to sell my fucking house?" I say my voice raised bordering at a yell

"Because that's what you do when you move Harper. You sell the old. What else would you do with it?" He asks in a condescending manner.

"I was going to let Jax have it. I mean he is the one who fucking paid for it. I thought it was only fair." I snap back at him.

"Why would he need it, doesn't he spend most of his time in jail anyway. I will never understand why you wasted your time with those people." He says with a disgust in his voice that I haven't noticed before, I was hurt by his opinion of them.

"Those people are my friends Tony. They took me in and were there for me when my parents weren't. They showed me what it was like to be a family." My voice was shaky and full of hurt. How the fuck could he say that shit, he knew what they were to me.

"I can give you a better family Harper, you know that. All they did was introduce you to drugs, crime and whatever disgusting fucked up shit Jax was into." His tone is sharp and there is almost a hint of jealousy wearing on his face.

"What the fuck is with you Tony?" I ask with tears running down my face.

"God dammit Harper, I know you have been fucking him again!" He said and I could hear the hurt in his voice.

"How did you find out?" I asked, without even wasting time trying to deny it.

"I saw the damn bite mark on the back of your shoulder, I'm sure you thought you hid it well, but I know I sure as hell didn't put it there. So, when I left this time, I decided I better figure something out" He confessed

"So, you thought your best solution was to pretend you didn't know, move me away and try to erase every trace of him?" I ask with anger at his actions and embarrassment at mine.

"I don't know Harper; I didn't want to lose you. I was hoping you got that fucking disgusting shit out of your system, but you aren't really acting like you have, so I guess I need to know right fucking now is, are you over him." He asks with a hint of desperation on his face. I stand there silent reflecting on the question and offended that he thinks any part of me is disgusting.

"I'm sorry Tony. I'm in love with him. I always have been" I confess through tears. The honesty feels good, but I do feel bad for hurting Tony.

"Well, I guess that's it then. I uh, I'll see myself out. Good luck Harper, you'll fucking need it." He says as he walks out

I feel a little bit of relief as he leaves, I knew moving wasn't the right choice and I was eventually going to back out. I know it was fucked up to lead Tony on like that, but I am in love with Jax, and I need to admit it. I am regretful that Tony found out in the way he did, I should have told him. Now I just need to figure out how to fix things with Jax, I said some pretty hurtful shit to him, I hope he will forgive me.

Chapter 13 Jax

I wake up to the feeling of being smacked in the back of my head.

"What the fuck!" I yell out looking up from my pillow to see who the hell hit me

"Oh, calm down son." My dad says. The bed groans as he sits down on the edge of it.

"What the hell dad?" I say a bit softer this time "What is it?"

"Well, your sister talked to me last night." He started to explain

"Dad, I don't wan..." He cut me off mid-sentence

"No, son you need to hear me. Now, you made your choices, and you got to live with them. So, it's time to man up a bit, get up and go get an honest Job. You owe that to her." He tells me and this is not really the conversation I wanted to have right now.

"It really doesn't matter anymore dad; Harper is moving to Seattle." I tell him trying to hide every bit of pain that brings me

"I know, but does she love him?" He questions knowing all too well the answer is no

"Ok dad, I'll talk to Kenny." I reassure him

SEATTLE, WHAT THE FUCK is she going to do in Seattle, I try shaking off the thoughts, but I just can't. I can't believe that Harper would fucking do that, especially after she just chewed

my ass for risking us being apart, prison would be temporary. I try to stay focused on my work, Kenny gave me the full-time position, and I really want to keep it. It's not great money but its honest money. It's not too bad, it's only been a couple weeks but so far so good. I just need to be able to concentrate on work and not let thoughts of Harper get in the way.

After I got the shop cleaned up for the night I headed up front to clock out when I heard Ricky's voice echoing through the shop and I froze at his words.

"Well holy fuck, Harper Kennedy, what brings you to this side of town again?" He laughs

"I-I was hoping to find Jax." she says nervously, and I make my way to the lobby

"What are you doing here Harper?" My words came out harsher than I meant them to but seriously, what the fuck did she want.

"I-I-I was...um...I was hoping to talk to you, please." she says stumbling over her words

"I'll give you two some privacy." Ricky says as he walks into the office.

"Look, Harper, if you're here to tell me you're moving I already know so please fucking spare me." I tell her coldly as I punch my number into the system to clock off

"Um, ya about that, I...um...I'm not going" she says softly

"Probably better, you wouldn't survive the city. So, you drove all the way over here to tell me that you're not moving to a place you never even told me you were moving to?" I question her. She has sparked my curiosity, but I am still annoyed by the whole situation

"Um, well not exactly, I-I wanted to say I'm sorry, I never should have said those things to you." She confesses and I can hear the remorse in her voice.

"I'm sorry too." I say offering my apology, I can tell she has more she wants to say but an awkward silence has filled the room

"What happened Harper?" I ask

"Um...Tony knows." she says with tears forming in her eyes

"Oh. When did he... I mean how did he..." I stumble over my question, I can't see Harper telling him, but I can't figure out how else for him to know

"He's known for a while now I guess, I didn't cover well enough, and he saw marks, he knew it wasn't from him because he thinks it's disgusting" she tells me as she wipes a tear away from her cheek

"I'm sorry Harper." I say softly. I am sorry and I feel bad for Harper, but I'm also amused by the thought of that fucker's face when he made the connection. I can't believe he didn't say anything though.

"It's on me Jax I made the choice. Anyway, I just wanted you to know that I broke up with him." she says as she works to calm her emotions. It takes me a minute to processes what she just said

"Wait, you broke up with him?" I ask confused, he catches her cheating, and she is the one to call it off.

"I'm in love with you Jax, I always have been. I had a fantasy about what the picture-perfect life would be or should be and it was wrong. You are my life, and I need you; the label doesn't make it real. I am so sorry." She barely gets the words out before I take her in my arms and crash my lips against hers. I am in love with her, and I have waited so long to get her back.

"I love you too Harper, I want to spend the rest of my life with you!" I confess to her, I'll fucking get married even, I just need her.

"Come home with me" she says almost commanding me to do so. It turns me on so fucking much there is no way I would even pretend to deny her.

Chapter 14 Harper

The table feels cold against my bare skin and the shackles are tight. My bare pussy aches for his touch as I lay here waiting, the silk blindfold is soft but takes away my ability to see where he's standing only adding to my arousal. I feel his fingertips start to caress my arms; it sends sparks through my body and makes my core heat. He runs his fingertips down my back, a small gasp escapes my lips and my heart beats wildly in my chest. The throbbing between my thighs grows more intense with each touch. I feel his lips gently kiss my thigh and I moan out with intensity as he kisses and nibbles closer and closer to my hot aching core.

I feel his hot breath at my folds "MORE" I beg; my words are replaced by moans as he sucks my clit into his mouth. He is relentless and it feels so fucking good. My legs quiver and my toes start to go numb; the shackles are the only things keeping me from falling. My moans turn to screams and pants as I find myself on the edge of release. His tongue swirls hard and fast circles on my swollen clit.

"Yes" I moan out "don't stop"

My pussy starts to clench around nothing as my arousal starts to drip, my body grows weak as my orgasm rips through it. I melt into the table as I try to catch my breath. I feel Jax lean over me, he places soft kisses on the crook of my neck

"Need a break baby cakes?" He whispers in that irresistible sexy voice.

I am out of breath and my clit is still sensitive, but I am so fucking ready for him to fuck me. I feel his hard dick pressing against my thigh and his hand wrapping up in my long hair, a breathy "no" is all I can manage to get out.

"Good" he groans, his voice full of desire.

He pulls my hair back and digs his other hand into my hip. With one hard thrust he slams into me, god he feels so fucking good. He keeps his pace steady and his thrusts hard just the way I like to start. Uncontrollable moans fall from my lips as his thrusts start to get harder and faster, his grip on my hair tightens as I feel the other hand release my hip only to land with a loud *smack* on my ass cheek.

"More" I scream out as he does it again and again. My pussy starts to clench around his dick as I feel myself getting close to the edge again.

"Be a good whore and cum for me baby cakes." He says, I feel my arousal drip and my body shake as I find my release at his words.

I fucking love it when he talks like that. I feel his body collapse onto mine as he finds his release. After a few breathless minutes I feel him undo the shackles, he takes off the blindfold and carries me to the bed. His lips mold to mine in a deep passionate kiss, I don't want it to end but he breaks it, I whimper a little at the loss but all he does is smirk. He walks to the bathroom, and I hear the bath water start to run, soon the aroma of sweet Lilly's and Jasmine fill the air.

When Jax returns he extends his hand out to me, and I accept it. He escorts me to the bath and helps me in; he plants a soft kiss on my forehead before leaving me in my candle lit bathroom. The bath feels so good I debate even getting out, but

I have been listening to Jax rummaging around in the kitchen and bedroom and my curiosity is killing me. When I come out of the bathroom I see Jax sitting on the bed, he had laid out a set of comfy pajamas for me, prepared a bowl of popcorn and had 2 beers on the nightstand.

"What's all this?" I ask with a smile

"It's Friday." He chuckles as he turns on the TV

My heart swells with Joy, he remembered. I put on my pajamas and crawled into bed next to him. He cupped my chin in his hand and gave me a soft kiss.

"I love you Harper. I always will." He says as he wraps his arm around me.

"I love you too Jax" I tell him as he hands me the bowl of popcorn. He picks a true crime documentary and hands me my beer. Title or no fucking title, I am happy, and I am never leaving this man again.

Don't miss out!

Visit the website below and you can sign up to receive emails whenever Melissa C publishes a new book. There's no charge and no obligation.

https://books2read.com/r/B-A-MKNCB-DNGVC

BOOKS2READ

Connecting independent readers to independent writers.

Did you love *Addicted To You*? Then you should read *Save Me*[1]
by Melissa C!

Kaylee Thomas spends her days bartending at a local tavern to pass the time. Living in a small town there really isn't much else to do. This is how she hopes people see it anyways. In reality it is an escape from the toxic hell she is trapped in. Kaylee's home life is growing more and more dangerous by the day, she desperately wants to escape the prison that it has become. With no real hope in sight Kaylee is afraid that her only out may be death. Her best friend Jason Peterson is desperate to save her before it is too late.

---

1. https://books2read.com/u/mZlAO2

2. https://books2read.com/u/mZlAO2

This book contains material that could be triggering for some people.

Read more at https://x.com/melissaC589024.

Also by Melissa C

Liquor and Lust
Addicted To You
Save Me

Watch for more at https://x.com/melissaC589024.

About the Author

I have always enjoyed writing steamy stories, but I have always viewed them as silly. I have always just deleted my work instead of finishing it, let alone publishing it. I finaly decided "What the heck, I love it so why not work on it" I enjoy the freedom self publishing brings me. I can write around my job, my kids, and our homestead. Between my full time job in caregiving, my 6 homeschooled children and all the chores, writing is my peace, my me time. I hope that my stories can bring entertainment to my readers because it brings me so much joy to write them.

Read more at https://x.com/melissaC589024.

About the Publisher

I love being an author and publisher all in one. I love the freedom of creating all my own material at my own pace.